The Mystery of the
Coon Cat

THREE COUSINS DETECTIVE CLUB®

The Mystery of the Coon Cat

Elspeth Campbell Murphy

Illustrated by Joe Nordstrom

BETHANY HOUSE PUBLISHERS

MINNEAPOLIS, MINNESOTA 55438

The Mystery of the Coon Cat
Copyright © 1999
Elspeth Campbell Murphy

Cover and story illustrations by Joe Nordstrom
Cover design by the Lookout Design Group

Scripture quotation is from the Bible in Today's English Version
(*Good News Bible*). Copyright © American Bible Society 1966,
1971, 1976, 1992

Published by Bethany House Publishers
A Ministry of Bethany Fellowship International
11400 Hampshire Avenue South
Minneapolis, Minnesota 55438
www.bethanyhouse.com

Printed in the United States of America by
Bethany Press International, Minneapolis, Minnesota 55438

Library of Congress Cataloging-in-Publication Data

Murphy, Elspeth Campbell.
    The mystery of the coon cat / by Elspeth Campbell Murphy.
       p. m . —(Three Cousins Detective Club ; 25)
    Summary: When he takes his neighbor's Maine coon cat to a
ceremony for the blessing of animals, Titus finds a mysterious note
in his pocket and with the help of his cousins determines its source.
    ISBN 0–7642–2133–7 (pbk.)
    [1. Maine coon cat—Fiction. 2. Cats—Fiction. 3. Cousins—
Fiction. 4. Mystery and detective stories.] I. Title. II. Series:
Murphy, Elspeth Campbell. Three Cousins Detective Club ; 25.
PZ7.M95316 Mxfe   1999   99–6561
[Fic]—dc21   CIP

ELSPETH CAMPBELL MURPHY has been a familiar name in Christian publishing for over twenty years, with more than one hundred books to her credit and sales approaching six million worldwide. She is the author of the bestselling series *David and I Talk to God* and *The Kids From Apple Street Church*, as well as the 1990 Gold Medallion winner *Do You See Me, God?*, and two books of prayer meditations for teachers, *Chalkdust* and *Recess*. A graduate of Trinity College and Moody Bible Institute, Elspeth and her husband, Mike, make their home in Chicago, where she writes full time.

Contents

"Lord, you have made so many things! How wisely you made them all! The earth is filled with your creatures."
Psalm 104:24

1

One Really Big Cat

"Yo! What is *that*?"

It was a question Titus McKay had heard before about Big Louie.

This time the question came from Titus's cousin Timothy Dawson, who was visiting Titus in the city. Timothy had just walked through the apartment doorway when he stopped dead in his tracks.

Titus's other cousin Sarah-Jane Cooper, who was right behind Timothy, slammed into him. But she didn't seem to notice. Instead, she just stared at Louie as if she couldn't believe her eyes.

"He's a cat," said Titus, trying hard to keep a straight face.

"Well, yes. I *know* he's a cat," said Timothy. "But . . . but—"

"But what *kind* of cat is he?" asked Sarah-Jane. "I've never seen anything like him before! He's *HUGE!*"

"He's a Maine coon cat," said Titus. "Pretty impressive, isn't he?"

"No kidding!" said Timothy. "What did you say he was?"

"A Maine coon," repeated Titus. "I think it's the biggest breed there is. And Louie is big even for a coon cat. He's plenty heavy. But he's not as heavy as people think he is. He just looks bigger because of all that fur and the long, bushy tail. Actually, that's how coon cats got their name. People thought they looked like raccoons."

"Or some kind of wild cat," said Sarah-Jane. "A—what do you call it? A lynx. He looks a little bit like a lynx."

"That, too," agreed Titus. "But you're not a wild cat, are you, Louie? No, you're not. You're just a big, old, fuzzy teddy bear, aren't you? Yes, you are!"

Titus nuzzled the cat's neck, and Louie rolled over to get his tummy rubbed.

Timothy and Sarah-Jane looked at each other in amazement. Since when had Titus McKay become a "cat person"?

Titus saw the looks on their faces and gave an embarrassed little cough. It was true that he had never been that crazy about cats. . . .

He tried to explain why Big Louie was so special.

"Maine coons are all-American cats," Titus said. "Their ancestors probably came over with the Pilgrims. Their fur is thick so they can survive rough New England winters."

Timothy and Sarah-Jane nodded politely. But they were still looking at him funny.

"Look, he's just a great cat, all right?" exclaimed Titus.

"Of course he is, Ti," said Sarah-Jane.

"Anything you say, Ti," said Timothy.

Titus sighed. For someone who wasn't that crazy about cats, he was crazy about this one.

Actually, Titus loved all kinds of animals. And all kinds of animals loved him.

He had a part-time job looking after animals in his apartment building when their owners were away. It was a lot of responsibility. But Titus liked animals so much it didn't even feel like work to take care of them.

Big Louie belonged to a neighbor who had just gotten a new job. Her job meant she had to travel a lot. Linda said if it hadn't been for Titus, she wouldn't have been able to keep Louie. And giving him away would have broken her heart.

So Titus and Big Louie had gotten to know each other really well. Louie even stayed over in Titus's apartment sometimes.

Today Big Louie was visiting for a special occasion—the Blessing of the Animals at the university.

When Linda found out she would have to be out of town and miss it, Titus volunteered to take Big Louie with them and bring back pictures for Linda.

Titus's little Yorkshire terrier, Gubbio, would never have let another dog near his boy. And Gubbio *really* wasn't crazy about cats. But for some reason, Gubbio and Big Louie got along OK. Gubbio seemed to understand that Louie was only visiting. And Louie seemed to think that Gubbio was just the cutest little thing.

Besides, Big Louie was a "doggy-ish" kind

of cat. He and Gubbio would team up and follow Titus all over the apartment. (Titus secretly thought this could get kind of annoying. But it was also sort of sweet, so he didn't want to say anything to them about it.)

Now they trotted along behind him when he went to the hall closet and got out their carriers.

Gubbio and Big Louie looked at each other in alarm.

Were they going to the *vet's*?

What was going on here?

"Relax!" Titus told them, as if he could read their minds. "You are *not* going to the vet's!"

2

All Creatures Great and Small

*I*t was a noisy trip.

Gubbio whined.

Big Louie yowled.

Apparently they didn't believe their human's story about not going to the vet's.

All over the visitors' parking lot at the university, people were lifting pet carriers out of their cars.

"Can we take Gubbio and Louie out of their carriers, Uncle Richard?" asked Sarah-Jane.

"I think we'd better!" said Titus's father. "If Gubbio and Louie are OK on the leash, we can just stash the carriers in the car."

"Will you guys relax?" Titus said as he let them out.

Gubbio and Louie looked around in happy surprise as if to say, "Hey! This isn't the vet's!"

Fortunately, both animals were well behaved on the leash. As a city cat, Louie mostly stayed indoors, of course, but Titus and Linda had taken him to the park a few times. And he had done amazingly well.

Titus looked around with interest. Most of the animals were dogs and cats. But he also spotted a couple of ferrets, several rabbits, a

turtle, and even an iguana. Then a van from the petting zoo unloaded a sheep, a goat, and a pig. Another van brought some dogs and cats from the animal shelter. There were even a couple of mounted police officers on their horses.

Suddenly, in all the excitement, Titus had the peculiar feeling that he was being watched.

Well, that isn't so unusual, Titus tried to tell himself. He was with Big Louie. And Big Louie always attracted a lot of attention.

But this was different somehow.

Quickly Titus looked around again. But he didn't see anyone in particular. And for the moment, the feeling passed.

3

The Blessing of the Animals

"**W**ow! There are so many people here!" Titus said.

"Right!" said his father. "Let's get a move on. The green is going to fill up pretty quickly."

They joined the crowds of people—and animals!—gathering outside the university chapel, which was actually a very large church. Pastors from many other churches were there, too.

A minister went up to the microphone and welcomed everyone—all the humans and their animal friends. Then he said a prayer, thanking God for all the wonderful things in the world, especially for the animals. He asked for God's help in taking care of them.

And then the choir sang a beautiful hymn about God's world.

> *All things bright and beautiful,*
> *All creatures great and small*
> *All things wise and wonderful:*
> *The Lord God made them all.*

After that it was time to get in line so that each animal could be prayed for one by one.

Titus's father glanced nervously at his watch. He had a meeting he couldn't get out of. And Titus's mother had had a ton of work to do at home, so she hadn't been able to come. "Are you kids going to be all right on your own for a little while?" he asked.

"We'll be fine, Dad," said Titus.

If there was one thing the cousins were proud of, it was that they could be trusted to be on their own without doing anything dumb or getting into trouble.

Titus's father knew this about them. He said good-bye and headed off to his meeting.

The cousins said good-bye and looked around for the shortest line.

But Sarah-Jane spotted a pet snake in that line and just about freaked out. She was not afraid of much of anything. But she definitely had a "thing" about snakes. And she had strong opinions about standing in line with them.

So the cousins moved on.

It was as they were looking for another line that Titus got the peculiar feeling again.

4

A Peculiar Feeling

"*T*hat's funny," said Titus.

"Funny ha-ha? Or funny weird?" asked Timothy.

"Funny weird," said Titus.

"What's funny weird?" asked Sarah-Jane. She sounded quite cheerful, now that her snake attack was over.

"I don't know," said Titus. "I just have this funny feeling that we're being watched."

"Of course we're being watched, Ti," said Timothy. "It's Big Louie. Haven't you noticed? He has a way of attracting attention."

Titus looked around him. Lots of people were glancing his way, smiling, murmuring, pointing at Louie. He even heard someone say, "Yo! What is *that*?"

20

But of course, he was used to that with Louie.

"No, it's not that," he said to his cousins, trying to explain the difference. "I just get the feeling that someone is watching us *on purpose.* Maybe even following us."

Timothy and Sarah-Jane looked around with new interest.

The cousins weren't scared. There were plenty of friendly people around—including police officers on their horses.

But it was still a peculiar feeling.

And there didn't seem to be anything they could do about it.

So they found a reptile-free line and settled in to wait their turn.

While they were waiting, Timothy decided to take a couple of practice pictures. So Titus picked up Big Louie. *Oof!* And Sarah-Jane picked up Gubbio.

They must have made a cute picture, because people started coming over to them to ask questions about Big Louie.

Titus explained patiently—

That the cat was a Maine coon.

That he weighed about sixteen pounds.

That he was almost four feet long from the tip of his nose to the tip of his tail.

That it wasn't Titus's cat.

That he had brought Louie as a favor to his neighbor Linda, who couldn't be there today.

That Linda had gotten Louie from a breeder when Louie was just a kitten.

That, yes, he agreed it was hard to imagine Louie as a kitten.

That he didn't know how much Louie cost, but that he knew Maine coon kittens were pretty expensive. Also, it depended on whether you wanted a show cat or just a great pet. Show cats always cost more.

"Wow!" muttered Titus when the people had finished petting Louie and finally wandered off. "Since when did I get to be a cat expert?"

5

Head of the Line

As the cousins were puzzling about this, the line moved forward. Suddenly, they were next.

"OK, how are we going to do this?" Titus asked. "Let's do Gubbio first."

"You should hold him, Ti," said Sarah-Jane. "He's your dog."

"Right," said Titus. This was a special moment for both of them. He set Louie down and gave the leash to Sarah-Jane.

Then he bent to pick up Gubbio. Gubbio felt light as air compared to Big Louie. "You're just the best dog in the world, aren't you?" Titus murmured in Gubbio's ear. Gubbio gave a happy little *woof*.

Now at the head of the line, Titus solemnly handed Gubbio to the minister, who said nice things about what a well-behaved dog he was.

"I've seen quite a few Yorkshire terriers today," the minister said with a smile. "They look alike. But each one is different and special."

He took Gubbio in his arms and said a lovely prayer for him. He asked that Titus's little dog would have a long and happy life with the boy who loved him and took care of him.

Timothy took a couple of Polaroids. The minister, the cousins, and Gubbio gathered around to see. The pictures came out great!

"I'm glad I took those practice shots earlier," Timothy said.

"We have one more animal," Titus told the minister. "He's not mine. He's my neighbor's. She couldn't be here today. But she really wanted Big Louie to come."

"Then it was very kind of you to bring him for her," said the minister.

Titus handed Gubbio to Sarah-Jane and bent down to—*oof!*—pick up Louie.

When the minister saw the cat, he didn't say, "Yo! What is *that*?" Instead he laughed right out loud and said, "Well, how about that!

It's a *Maine coon*! The first one I've seen today!
Isn't he a beauty?"

"Yes!" said Sarah-Jane. "He's a *great* cat!
Right, Louie?" She nuzzled Louie's neck the
way Titus had done. "You're just a sweet,
sweet, beautiful, big, BIG kitty!"

Big Louie meowed as if to say that he
couldn't agree more, and everyone laughed.

Then the minister said a prayer for Big
Louie, and Timothy took pictures to give to
Linda.

The cousins thanked the minister and

moved out of the way so that the little girl behind them in line could come up with her hamster.

"Wow!" exclaimed Timothy as they wandered off. "That was neat-O!"

"So cool," agreed Sarah-Jane as she and Titus set Gubbio and Big Louie down.

Even the animals seemed to sense that something special had happened to them.

"It was EX-cellent!" said Titus, reaching into his pocket to get out treats for the animals. "Even nicer than I thought it would be. . . ."

Immediately, Titus whipped his hand out again.

"What's the matter, Ti?" asked Timothy innocently. "Did the snake in your pocket bite you?"

"Not even remotely funny, Tim!" snapped Sarah-Jane.

"No, not a snake," said Titus, holding out his hand, which was shaking a little. "This!"

6

A Mysterious Message

*T*imothy and Sarah-Jane just stared at him blankly as Titus held out a piece of folded paper.

"What's that?" asked Sarah-Jane.

"I don't know," said Titus.

"What do you mean you don't know?" asked Timothy.

Timothy and Sarah-Jane glanced at each other. Titus was known for carrying a lot of stuff around in his pockets. But he was also rather picky about it. He always knew what he had with him.

"I mean—I don't know because it's not mine," said Titus. "I didn't put it there when I loaded up my pockets this morning."

"Then how did it get there?" asked Sarah-Jane.

All Titus could do was shrug.

It was a mystery.

Fortunately, the cousins were good at solving mysteries. They even had a detective club.

Titus said, "It looks like someone somehow managed to slip a note in my pocket without me knowing it. Maybe it happened when everybody was crowding around to see Louie." He paused as a new thought struck him. "You know that funny feeling I had that we were being followed?"

Timothy and Sarah-Jane nodded.

"Maybe it was real," said Titus. Maybe someone *was* following us around—just to give us this."

He paused and gave an embarrassed little laugh. "And—since we're such great detectives—maybe we should unfold it and read it. What do you think?"

Timothy and Sarah-Jane couldn't help laughing, too. Sometimes it was easy to overlook the obvious—even for detectives.

They had been so puzzled about *how* the paper had gotten into Titus's pocket that they had forgotten to see *what* it said.

Titus unfolded the note, and the three detective cousins crowded around to read it.

It was written in cursive, but it wasn't too hard to read. The first two lines were written neatly in black ink. The third line was scrawled in blue ink.

Be careful at the cat show!
They're planning to steal your cat.
Warn Linda!

7

Questions

*T*hat was all.

No clue as to who had written the note.

No clue as to who the thieves might be.

But it was the message itself that Titus didn't understand. That is to say, he *understood* it. He just didn't know what it *meant*.

"Steal Louie?" yelped Sarah-Jane, who had gotten quite fond of Titus's cat friend. "That's horrible! You definitely have to tell your neighbor, Ti!"

"Oh, I will," said Titus. "Definitely. Except . . ."

"Except what, Ti?" asked Timothy. "You look as if something doesn't make sense."

As a matter of fact, a lot of things didn't make sense. Thoughts were swirling around in

Titus's head so fast, it was hard to get the questions straightened out—let alone the answers!

Timothy and Sarah-Jane waited patiently.

It was a rule they had in their detective club. If one cousin was trying to get his or her thoughts together, the other cousins had to be quiet and wait.

Finally Titus said, "OK, here's the thing. Big Louie isn't a show cat."

Timothy and Sarah-Jane looked at him as if to say he needed to try a little harder to get his thoughts together!

Titus tried again. "OK. Louie is a pure-bred. But that just means that all of his ancestors were Maine coons. It doesn't mean that he's perfect."

"Nobody's perfect," said Sarah-Jane.

Titus glanced down at Louie. Louie looked back up as if he knew people were talking about him.

"Don't get me wrong," Titus said quickly. "Louie is a great cat. A *great* cat! But he's not what they call 'show-quality.' A show cat has to be *outstanding*. You and I might not be able to tell the differences, but judges can. When people take their cats to shows, judges pick the best of each breed. And you can't just waltz in and win a prize. It takes *a lot* of time and work to show your cat."

Timothy frowned thoughtfully. "I don't get it. If Louie isn't a show cat, and Linda doesn't have tons of time because of her job, then why would she be taking Louie to a cat show?"

"She wouldn't!" said Titus.

"But if she's *not* going to the cat show," said Sarah-Jane, "then why would someone warn her that some other people are planning to steal her cat there? Either way, it doesn't make sense!"

8

Another Tabby?

"*T*he minister knew right away that Big Louie was a Maine coon," said Titus slowly.

Timothy shrugged. "Well, sure. If he'd seen one before, he'd know it if he saw another one."

"That's what I'm getting at," said Titus. "Animals of the same breed all look alike. It's that way with Yorkshire terriers. You know one when you see one."

Timothy and Sarah-Jane just looked at him. The cousins had a rule that you couldn't say "Duh!" when another cousin said something really obvious.

Titus could tell that Timothy and Sarah-Jane were having a hard time keeping that rule.

He tried again. "Here's what I'm getting at.

Maine coons look alike, too. Granted, they can be lots of different colors. But they're basically the same size and shape. And the most popular marking is light and dark brown stripes. A tabby. Like Louie."

Timothy and Sarah-Jane were listening closely now. "Go on," they said.

"Well," said Titus. "I've been trying to remember something the minister said. And I finally have it."

"Go on," said Timothy and Sarah-Jane.

"Well," said Titus. "When the minister saw Gubbio, he said he'd seen quite a few Yorkshire terriers today. But when he saw Louie, he said it was the *first* Maine coon he'd seen today."

"Meaning. . . ?" said Timothy.

"Meaning that *we've* been acting as if Louie is the *only* Maine coon at the Blessing of the Animals," said Titus.

Sarah-Jane said, "So—just because we haven't *seen* another coon cat, doesn't mean there's not another coon cat here."

"That's what I'm saying," said Titus.

"And if there's another coon cat here," said Timothy, "chances are it's a brown tabby like

Louie. You said that was the most popular kind."

Titus nodded. "It's perfectly possible that there's another brown tabby coon cat here today. Except—what if *that* tabby is a show cat?"

9

The Warning

*T*he cousins gathered round to look at the mysterious note again.

> *Be careful at the cat show!*
> *They're planning to steal your cat.*
> *Warn Linda!*

Sarah-Jane said, "Why is part of it written in black ink and part of it written in blue ink? The two parts don't look like they go together."

"The two parts don't *sound* like they go together, either," added Timothy. "The first part says *your* cat. But the second part says to warn *Linda*—as if it's not 'your' cat. It doesn't make sense."

Titus said, "What if someone knew that some people were planning to steal a valuable Maine coon cat at a cat show?

"And what if this person thought that the cat's owner would be here today at the Blessing of the Animals?

"And what if this person came here to warn the owner?

"But what if he wanted it to be a *secret* kind of warning?

"He might write a note ahead of time that says: *'Be careful at the cat show! They're planning to steal your cat.'*

"And he might bring the note, figuring he'll just slip it into her pocket or something."

Timothy said, "But when he gets here, the only Maine coon he sees is with some kids. Us."

"And that's why he followed us?" asked Sarah-Jane. "Because we were the only ones with a Maine coon?"

"Maybe he didn't know what else to do," said Titus. Maybe he thought we were watching the cat for the owner or something."

"Well, that much is true," said Timothy.

"We *were* watching the cat for someone. Linda."

Sarah-Jane added, "So maybe this person was hanging around when all those people were asking you about Maine coons, Ti. And maybe he heard you say that you were taking care of the cat for your neighbor—*Linda*. So he figured he had the right person."

Titus said, "So he gets out the note he was planning to give to Linda. And he adds *'Warn Linda!'* to it with the only pen he has handy.

"And then he does what he had planned to do all along. He slips the warning into a pocket. Only it's *my* pocket. I was supposed to find the note and pass it along to Linda."

Sarah-Jane said, "The only problem is—he got the wrong cat."

"And the wrong Linda," said Timothy.

"Which means," said Titus, "that somewhere around here there's a person named Linda. Her Maine coon show cat is in danger. And she doesn't know it. She didn't get the warning. *We* did."

10

Another Linda?

The cousins looked around them. The crowds were thinning out a little, but not by much.

New people were still getting in line.

But the people who had already been in line weren't leaving. The cousins couldn't leave, of course, because they had to wait for Titus's father.

But these other people just seemed to be having too good a time to go home. Pet owners stood about in little groups, chatting happily with other pet owners.

Timothy said it reminded him of when his parents took his baby sister, Priscilla, to the park. They met up with other parents—even people they didn't know—and everyone stood around talking about their babies.

"So," said Titus. "In the middle of all these happy people talking about their pet babies, is there someone named Linda?"

Sarah-Jane said, "It's a pretty popular name. I'd be more surprised if there *isn't* someone here named Linda. But it could be that the Linda we're thinking of didn't come today at all. Or maybe she came late. Maybe that's why the note writer didn't see her."

"Someone named Linda who has a cat that looks like Louie," said Timothy, stating the situation.

The cousins all looked down.

Another cat that looked like Louie? That didn't seem possible. But of course, it *was* possible. It was more than possible. There were probably *thousands* of cats all over the country who looked liked Louie.

"Look at it this way," said Titus. "*If* there's someone named Linda here, who has a cat who looks like this guy, it's going to make it a lot easier to find her."

Sarah-Jane and Timothy nodded. And of course they had to find her and warn her that her cat was in danger. They had decided that without even talking it over.

If there was even the chance that they could help, didn't they have to take it?

So what if the note writer couldn't find the right person? That didn't mean *they* couldn't.

After all, they were detectives, weren't they? How hard could it be?

11

The Search

*P*lenty hard.

Even though they had a lot of ground to cover, the cousins knew that they couldn't split up to look for the cat.

This was because they had a rule that said when the three of them were out on their own, they had to stay together.

This wasn't a rule of their detective club. It was a rule their parents had given them.

It worked on the honor system, of course. After all, if they were on their own, their parents weren't there to check up on them. But the cousins figured that's when obeying the rules really counted most—when there was no one there to make you obey.

So they stuck together and set off to look

for the mysterious cat that might not even be there.

They tried to be methodical about it. Instead of running every which way, they decided to walk slowly around the edge of the green, trying to see as much as they could. If that didn't work, they planned to walk back and forth through the crowds.

They didn't know what else to do.

When it came to the search, Gubbio wasn't much help. But he wasn't a problem, either. He was just happy to be with his people and to be out for a walk.

Big Louie was another story. He was sort of helpful and sort of not.

The way he was not helpful was that he suddenly sat down and refused to budge. It was as if he had decided that walking was for the dogs.

But he was helpful, because when Titus carried him—*oof!*—he got a lot more attention. People could just see him better.

And whenever people noticed Louie, the cousins asked if they had seen another cat there today that looked just like him.

A few people looked at the cousins as if

they were crazy. Another cat who looked like *that*?

But everyone was very nice.

Even though no one had seen another Maine coon cat.

So it was hard not to get discouraged. They had been so sure they were right about Linda and her cat. Why couldn't they find them?

"We're getting nowhere fast," sighed Titus. "Let's take a break."

He stopped at a drinking fountain, put Louie down, and pulled a plastic dish from his jacket pocket. (Titus liked to come prepared.)

He filled the dish with water from the drinking fountain and set it on the ground. Gubbio and Louie took turns drinking from it.

Then the cousins got drinks of water from the fountain themselves.

Titus was just about to put the dish away when he felt something nudge him gently in the back.

He turned around and jumped back in surprise. Then he broke into a huge smile. He was used to animals coming up to him all the time. But they weren't usually this big!

He was face-to-face with a huge police horse.

"Sparky!" laughed the police officer. "What are you doing? Don't bother these kids!"

"He's not bothering me," said Titus, also laughing. "He's a great horse, aren't you, Sparky? I think he just wants a drink of water, Officer."

"I think you're right," the policeman replied.

So Titus filled up the dish with water and

held it out to Sparky. It took quite a few refills!

And then Gubbio and Louie decided that they were still thirsty. Either that or they just decided that they didn't want some big old horse getting all the attention.

It was when Titus was putting the dish down that the policeman noticed Big Louie for the first time.

"Yo!" he said. "What is *that*?"

12
The T.C.D.C.

*T*he cousins looked at one another. Of course! Why hadn't they thought of this before?

"Officer, we need to talk to you about a robbery," said Titus.

The policeman (whose name was Officer Simons) looked at them in surprise.

"You want to report a robbery?"

"No," said Titus. "We want to *prevent* a robbery."

It took a while—quite a while—to explain to the policeman what they thought was going on.

"So you don't know what this woman Linda looks like?" asked Officer Simons.

"No," said Sarah-Jane. "We just think she has a cat that looks like Louie."

Officer Simons looked at Louie with raised eyebrows. "Doesn't seem that a cat this big should be so hard to find."

"That's what we thought," said Timothy. "But we've been searching pretty hard, and we haven't come up with anything yet."

"It's nice of you to go to all this trouble," said the policeman.

"We like to do this kind of thing," Sarah-Jane replied. "We're the T.C.D.C."

"What's a 'teesy-deesy'?" asked Officer Simons.

Titus felt a little shy about explaining to a real policeman that he and his cousins had a detective club. But he did it anyway. Sometimes you just can't let shyness get in your way.

"It's letters," he explained. "Capital T. Capital C. Capital D. Capital C. It stands for the Three Cousins Detective Club."

"Detectives?" the officer replied. "That's great!" He sounded as if he really meant it, which was nice—especially coming from a professional.

"Tell you what," said Officer Simons. "You kids keep looking on foot. And my partner and

I will ride around and see if we see another Maine coon."

The cousins could hardly keep from jumping up and down. (But they didn't, because they didn't think they would look like serious detectives if they did.)

This was fantastic! A real live policeman believed their story and was offering to help them! They had been getting pretty discouraged. But now they were eager to start looking again.

Officer Simons said, "It might help if we could find the note writer, too. He—or she—might have left right after you got the note. But if this person is still around, I'd like to ask him what's going on. You didn't happen to get a look at this person?"

Titus shook his head, feeling a little embarrassed again. *Some detective!* he thought. *A person can come right up to you and slip a note in your pocket and you don't even notice him. Let alone get a description.*

"We didn't even see it happen," sighed Sarah-Jane, echoing what Titus was thinking. "So we have no idea what the note writer looks like."

"No," said Timothy. "But I might have a picture of him."

13

Photographs

Everyone stared at Timothy.

He reached in his pocket and brought out an envelope of pictures.

Titus, Sarah-Jane, and Officer Simons gathered around as Timothy began spreading out the pictures on the grass.

"These are very good!" said Officer Simons, sounding a little surprised that a kid could take such good pictures.

"Thank you," said Timothy. "Taking pictures is something I really like to do. We promised Linda—Ti's neighbor, that is—that we would bring back pictures of Louie. So these photographs are of the minister and Gubbio and Louie when it was our turn in line.

"But I wanted to make sure they would

come out. So I took some practice shots earlier."

Timothy spread out the rest of the pictures.

He said, "It was when Ti and S-J were
holding Louie and Gubbio that people started
crowding around. Mostly they wanted to ask
about Louie. We think that's when the note
writer saw his chance to warn us. As you can
see, there are a lot of extra people in these
practice shots. Maybe one of them is the note
writer."

They all bent over the photographs and studied them carefully.

There were so many people in the pictures, how could they ever tell who was who?

"There!" said Titus suddenly.

He pointed at a young man in the background. There was nothing unusual-looking about him. He had blond hair and was wearing jeans, a T-shirt, and a denim jacket.

"He's not holding a pet," said Titus. "Everyone else either has a pet or is with someone who has a pet. He's kind of off by himself with no animal around. Tim, do you have any other pictures of this guy?"

Timothy shuffled through the pile and found a picture with a closer shot of the young man.

He was holding something in his hand. Something square and white.

"The note?!" squeaked Sarah-Jane.

"Could be," said Officer Simons. "It's kind of hard to tell for sure."

Titus sighed. "That's the way it's been all day. Could be there's another tabby who looks like Louie. But we don't know for sure. Could be there's another Linda who's going to get her cat stolen. But we don't know for sure. Could be this guy is the note writer. But we don't know for sure."

"That's the way it often is with police work," said Officer Simons. "There's just one thing I know for sure."

"What's that?" asked Titus.

Officer Simons grinned. "Sparky wants his picture taken with you guys."

14

An Important Announcement

*I*t was fun getting their picture taken with Sparky. What a great horse!

Then Timothy gave Officer Simons and his partner a photograph of the note writer. And the cousins kept the other one. No one thought they'd really find the guy, but it didn't hurt to be prepared.

And of course, no one needed a picture of Louie to tell what a Maine coon brown tabby looked like. Once you'd seen Big Louie, it was hard to forget him.

So the cousins set off and the search was on again.

Titus said, "If Linda's here, why haven't we

spotted her? I just have this feeling that we're overlooking something. Something simple."

"What?" asked Sarah-Jane.

"I have no idea," said Titus.

And he had no time to think about it, because just then Louie got into an argument with another cat, and Titus had to haul him away.

Such yowling!

"Be quiet, Louie!" Titus said sternly. "I thought we agreed when I took you out of the pet carrier that you would behave on your leash. Now you just settle . . ."

Titus suddenly looked up at his cousins. "That's it!"

"What's it?" asked Timothy.

"That's why we haven't spotted the other tabby!" said Titus. "Not everyone is such a baby about riding in a pet carrier as these guys."

Gubbio and Louie looked around to see which guys he was talking about.

"Of course!" said Sarah-Jane. "We've been looking for the *cat*! But what if Linda has the cat in a *carrier*? If it's a show cat, it would be used to riding in a carrier, wouldn't it?"

The cousins looked around. There were lots of people with pet carriers.

Lots and lots of pet carriers.

How would they ever find the right one?

Titus said, "Let's find Officer Simons. I have an idea."

It was not that big a deal to find a police horse. But the cousins were still pleased with themselves when they hooked up with him almost right away. It felt good to be able to find *something*.

Titus explained to the police about the pet carrier and about his idea.

Officer Simons and his partner agreed that it was certainly worth a try.

Together they found the minister who had said the opening prayer. They told him what they needed, and he agreed to help.

He went back to the microphone and said, "May I have your attention, please? Will Linda, the owner of a Maine coon cat, please come to the chapel steps? Linda, the owner of a Maine coon cat. It's very important."

Of course, everyone on the whole green turned toward the microphone.

Titus found himself trying to hide behind Sparky. If this didn't work, he was going to be seriously embarrassed.

15

Louisa May Alcott

*T*here were a few tense moments when nothing happened.

Then Titus saw a middle-aged lady hurrying toward the chapel steps.

In her hands she held a large pet carrier. On her face she wore a worried expression. Especially when she saw the police.

Titus had been thinking so much about his neighbor Linda that it took him a minute to realize what was going on. Just because the cats looked alike didn't mean the owners had to.

Before anyone could ask, the woman said, sounding puzzled, "I'm Linda. I have a Maine coon cat. I just got here a little while ago. May I ask what this is about?"

Officer Simons said, "Your cat is a show cat, is that right, ma'am?"

"Yes," said Linda, sounding proud now—if still puzzled. "She's an award winner!"

She opened the pet carrier and brought out an exquisitely beautiful brown tabby coon cat.

The cat was smaller than Louie and "fancier" somehow. But unless you saw them together, it would be easy to mix them up.

"This is Louisa May Alcott," said Linda. She's named after one of my favorite authors."

"Mine, too!" exclaimed Sarah-Jane.

Linda smiled. "Of course, I don't call her that all the time. Mostly I just call her Loui."

The cousins looked at one another. The *same name*?? How weird was *that*?

Just then Big Louie let out a big meow, and Linda gasped. She hadn't seen him down there behind Titus.

"This guy is called Louie, too," said Titus. "Except he's not a show cat. Anyway, we think someone may have given us a warning by mistake. We think the warning may have been meant for you."

"A *warning*?!" cried Linda. "For *me*? What about? Oh, dear! Not about *Loui*!"

Officer Simons held out the photograph Timothy had given him. "Do you recognize the young man in this picture, ma'am?"

"Yes," said Linda. "I mean, I don't *know* him. I don't even know his name. But I've *seen* him before. I think he's a relative or a friend of some people I've met at the cat shows."

The cousins glanced at one another. Aha! This was finally beginning to make sense!

"But what's all this about a warning?" asked Linda.

"We've been looking all over for you," said Titus. "We wanted to give you this."

He handed her the note.

Linda read it in alarm.

Titus said, "We think the guy in the picture came here to warn you that someone was going to steal your cat."

"And you think it's these people from the cat show?" asked Linda.

Titus shrugged. "The note doesn't say who. But the guy had a kind of sneaky way of giving the warning. Just slipping a note in someone's pocket. It was like he wanted you to know what was going to happen. But he didn't want anyone to know who told you."

"I can't believe it!" gasped Linda. "What a terrible, terrible crime!"

"Well, that's just it, ma'am," said Officer Simons. "No crime has been committed. You have the note writer to thank for that. And these kids here—the Three Cousins Detective Club."

"Detectives!" exclaimed Linda, sounding very impressed. "Oh, thank you all *so* much! You can be sure that I won't take my eyes off Louisa May Alcott for one minute at the cat show! Now, if you'll excuse me, I need to get back in line. Being at the Blessing of the Animals means so much to Loui, I can't tell you!"

As Linda hurried away, Officer Simons smiled and said, "People sure can get crazy over their pets, can't they?"

"Hey," said Titus with a shrug. "What can I tell you? It happens."

He smiled down at Gubbio and Louie.

Titus knew it wasn't possible, but he could have sworn they winked at him.

The End

Series for Young Readers*
From Bethany House Publishers

★ ★ ★

THE ADVENTURES OF CALLIE ANN
by Shannon Mason Leppard

Readers will giggle their way through the true-to-life escapades of Callie Ann Davies and her many North Carolina friends.

★ ★ ★

BACKPACK MYSTERIES
by Mary Carpenter Reid

This excitement-filled mystery series follows the mishaps and adventures of Steff and Paulie Larson as they strive to help often-eccentric relatives crack their toughest cases.

★ ★ ★

THE CUL-DE-SAC KIDS
by Beverly Lewis

Each story in this lighthearted series features the hilarious antics and predicaments of nine endearing boys and girls who live on Blossom Hill Lane.

★ ★ ★

RUBY SLIPPERS SCHOOL
by Stacy Towle Morgan

Join the fun as home-schoolers Hope and Annie Brown visit fascinating countries and meet inspiring Christians from around the world!

★ ★ ★

THREE COUSINS DETECTIVE CLUB®
by Elspeth Campbell Murphy

Famous detective cousins Timothy, Titus, and Sarah-Jane learn compelling Scripture-based truths while finding—and solving—intriguing mysteries.

* (ages 7–10)